DEDICATION
This book is dedicated to the little white dog who helped so many children when they were sick and to all the other dogs of the world who share their lives and their hearts with those of us who reach out to them.

ACKNOWLEDGMENTS
I would like to thank Charise Neugebauer for her help in editing the manuscript. I am especially delighted by the warm and tender illustrations by Julie Litty. They come from her heart and bring to this book a true message of the power of unconditional love. Finally, my grateful thanks to Michael Neugebauer, my true friend, who also happens to be my publisher.

AUTHOR'S NOTE
This book is based on a true story about a little white dog who was adopted by a children's hospital in London, and whose love and affection for the young patients there helped in their recoveries. The events in this story took place long ago. Since then animals are increasingly used in this manner, but of course under far more stringent guidelines that include sanitary precautions and extensive training and supervision of service dogs. This use of animals is just one aspect of what is known as pet-assisted therapy, which grew out of research into the bond between animals and humans. As a result of this research, it was discovered that the love and companionship of animals can significantly contribute to sick people's recovery and rehabilitation. Pet-assisted therapy encompasses more than helping critically ill children as in *Dr. White*. Many dedicated individuals and organizations around the world are using this animal-human bond for a wide range of problems—including work with the elderly, the disabled, the mentally ill—and studies continue to be done on the general health benefits that pets can offer humans.

When I learned about Dr. White and the comfort he gave to countless suffering children, I thought his story would be a wonderful one to share. I hope children will share it with their parents.

Text copyright © 1999 by Jane Goodall
Illustrations copyright © 1999 by Nord-Süd Verlag AG

First published in the United States, Great Britain, Canada, Australia, and New Zealand in 1999 by North-South Books, an imprint of Nord-Süd Verlag AG, Gossau Zürich, Switzerland.

Distributed in the United States by North-South Books Inc., New York.

Library of Congress Cataloging-in-Publication Data is available.
A CIP catalogue record for this book is available from the British Library.
ISBN 0-7358-1063-X (trade binding) 10 9 8 7 6 5 4 3 2 1
ISBN 0-7358-1064-8 (library binding) 10 9 8 7 6 5 4 3 2 1
Printed in Belgium

For more information about our books, and the authors and artists who create them, visit our web site: http://www.northsouth.com

Jane Goodall
Dr. White

Illustrated by Julie Litty

A MICHAEL NEUGEBAUER BOOK

NORTH-SOUTH BOOKS / NEW YORK / LONDON

It was a cold, wet morning.
Dr. White dashed to the hospital. He was late.
He slipped through the back door of the kitchen.

The cook saw Dr. White first. Without saying a word, she grabbed a towel and dried his shaggy head.

"Where have you been? I saved your breakfast, but you'd better hurry. Mark was worse during the night. The nurses have already been down here asking for you."

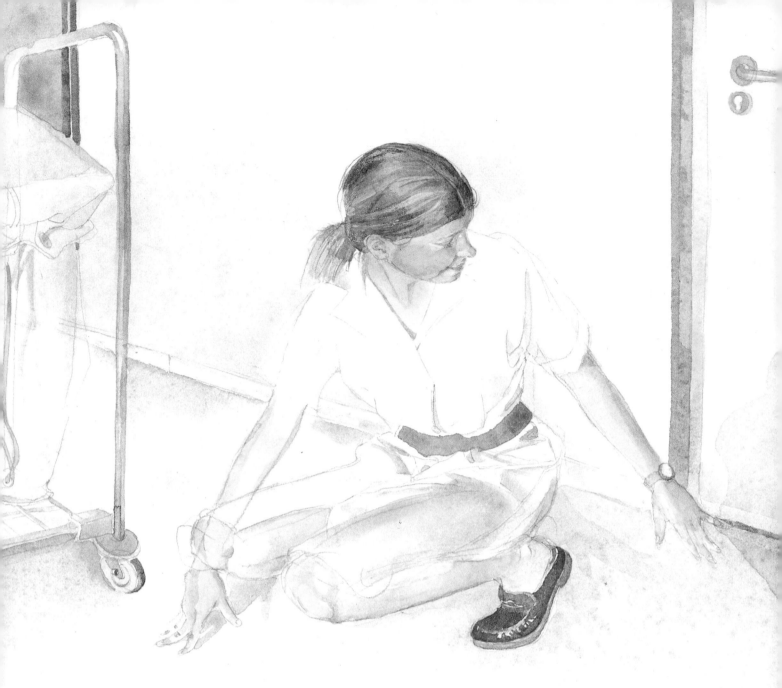

Dr. White quickly slurped his warm tea with cream and sugar and hastily gobbled his buttered toast.
Without wiping his mouth, he ran up two flights of stairs and down the hall on the left.
Several nurses and doctors greeted him as he passed.

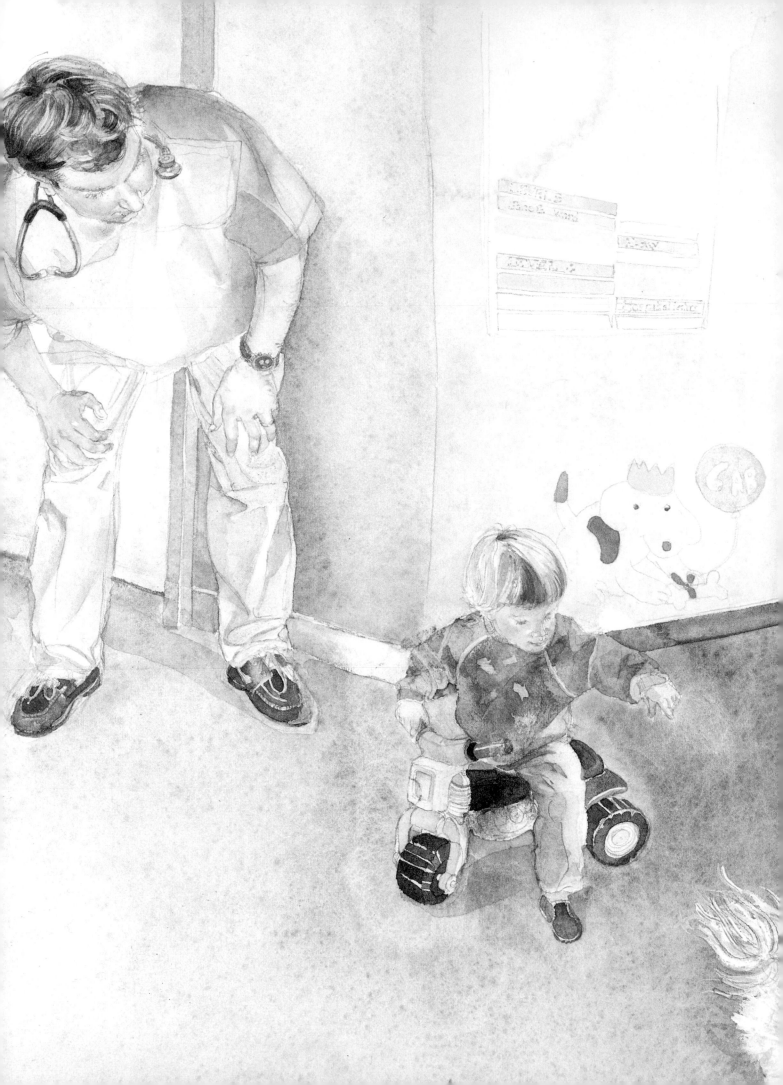

Dr. White paused in the doorway before entering. Mark's face was pale. His eyes were closed and he lay motionless. Mark's mother was sitting by his bed and crying.

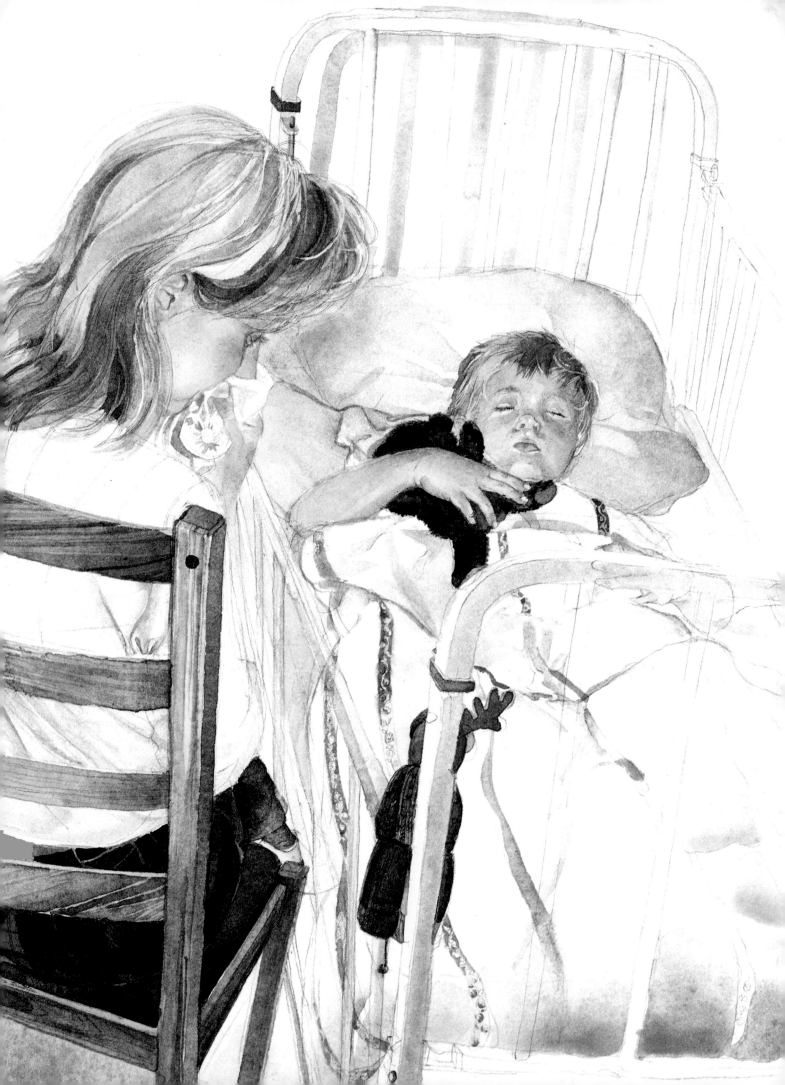

When Mark's mother saw Dr. White enter the room, she smiled with relief. Dr. White jumped on the bed and curled up close to Mark. He licked Mark's hand to let him know he was there.
Mark opened his eyes halfway and smiled.
Mark's mother relaxed. She believed in Dr. White's tail-wagging treatment. She kissed her son and patted Dr. White on the head.

"Look after him for me," she said. Then she left them alone.

Day after day the little white dog
visited the wards of the hospital.
He wagged his tail and looked
at the children with his
soft brown eyes. Sometimes
he nudged them with his
cold black nose.
He always seemed
to know when a child
was critically ill.

Then, he would jump on the bed
and curl up close to them. He would lie
there for hours, gently licking their
hand and thumping his tail.

One day as Dr. White was making his rounds,
he passed a man with a very red face.
The man began screaming for the nurse.
"There's a dog in the ward! There's a dog!!"

The ward nurse quickly tried to explain.
"He's a very special dog. He has saved many lives!"

The man turned out to be the health inspector and he wouldn't listen
to a word of the nurse's explanation.
He reported the hospital immediately.
It was official. Dr. White was no longer allowed to visit his patients.

Day after day, the little white dog curled up on the step outside the door to the hospital kitchen. His brown eyes were sad and he never wagged his tail.

The children missed him. Many of them weren't getting better, and some were getting worse. Mark had been one of the lucky ones. Dr. White had worked his magic on him. He had recovered and gone home.

Months after Mark had left the hospital,
the health inspector returned.
The head nurse met him in the
hallway.
"I suppose you're here to snoop
again?" she said bitterly.
"Well, you needn't worry.
The dog doesn't come in
here anymore and my
patients are suffering."
She looked at the inspector
and saw tears rolling down
his cheeks.
"I'm afraid my little girl
is terribly sick." His voice
cracked. "Won't you
please come and see her?"
The nurse followed him
down the hall to the ward
where the sickest
children were cared for.

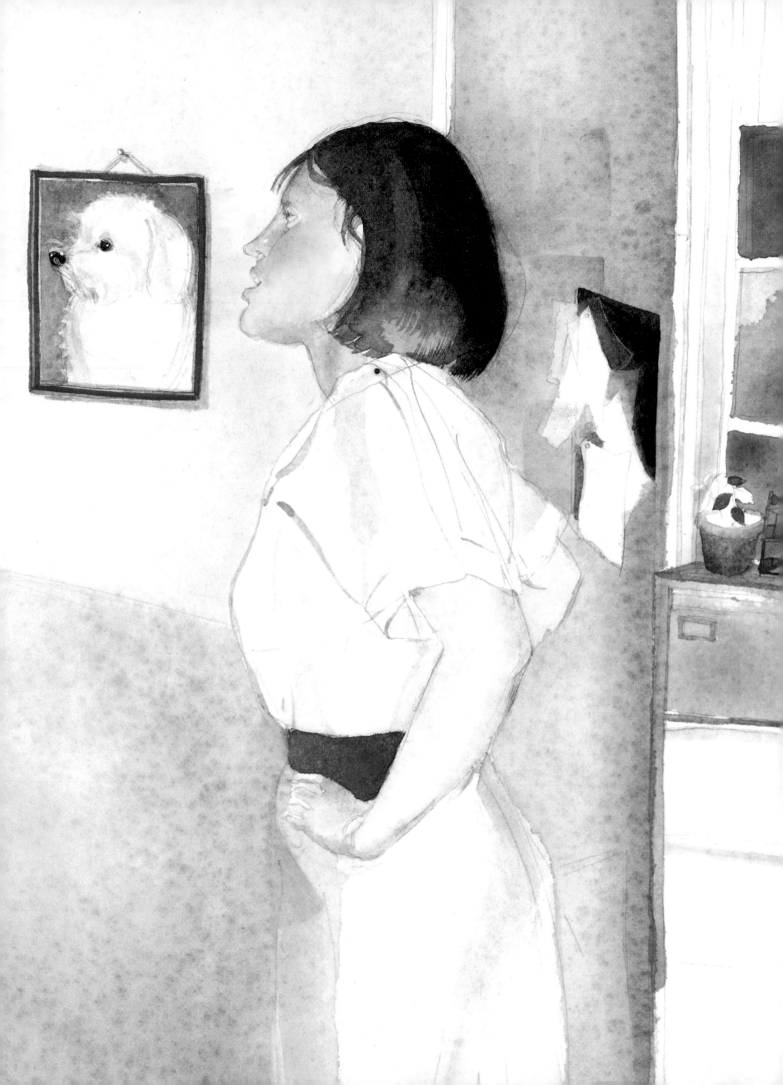

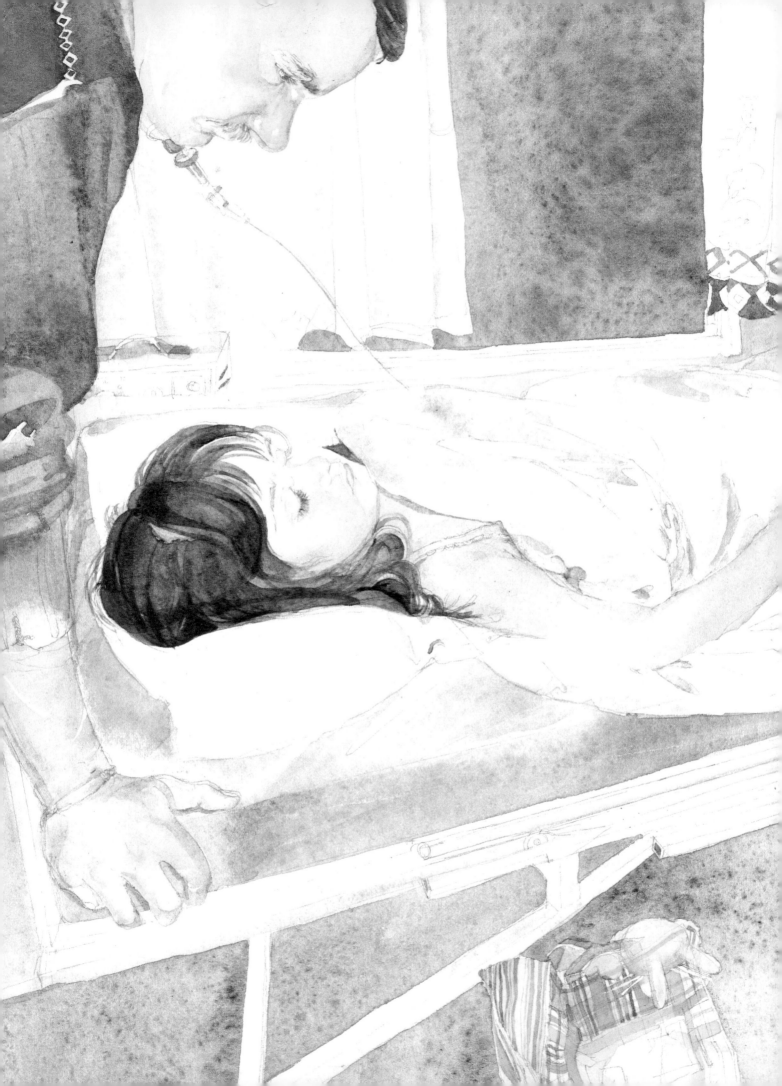

There lay a beautiful child.
Her father spoke to her, but she did not open her eyes.
"Please get better. I need you," he pleaded as his tears fell onto the child's
face. The little girl didn't move. She didn't respond to his words.
The head nurse thought about Mark. He had lain in this same room.
Day after day, the little white dog had curled up beside him. Slowly,
miraculously, Mark had recovered. The nurse looked at the distressed
father. "We'll do all we can for your daughter," she said.

That night, the nurse went down to the kitchen.
She opened the back door.
Dr. White was curled up on the step.
His brown eyes were sad, but he gave her a little
welcome with his tail.
She held the door open, inviting him inside.
He leapt up and trotted through the kitchen.
Up two flights, down the hall.

Dr. White stood in the doorway of the little
girl's room. Her face was pale.
Her eyes were closed and she lay motionless.
Dr. White jumped on the bed and curled up
close to her. His cold black nose touched her
hand, but she still didn't move.
He gently licked her hand from time to time
to let her know he was there.

The next morning when the health
inspector entered the hospital room,
he saw his daughter curled up next
to the little white dog. As Dr. White
thumped his tail, the little girl opened
her eyes and smiled at her father.
Reaching out to stroke the little white
dog, the health inspector thanked him
for restoring his daughter's health.

No one will ever know how many lives the little white dog saved,
but a story is told that it was the health inspector himself who moved
Dr. White's bowl back into the kitchen.